YUYI MOR...

Little Night
Nochecita

SQUARE
FISH

A NEAL PORTER BOOK
ROARING BROOK PRESS

As the long day comes to an end, Mother Sky fills a tub with falling stars and calls, "Bath time for Little Night!"

Little Night answers from afar. "Can't come. I am hiding and you have to find me, Mama. Find me now!"

Cuando llega el final de un largo día, Madre Cielo llena la bañera de estrellas fugaces y anuncia:

—¡Es hora de bañar a Nochecita!

Nochecita contesta desde lejos.

—No puedo ir. Estoy escondida y tienes que encontrarme, Mami. ¡Ven a buscarme!

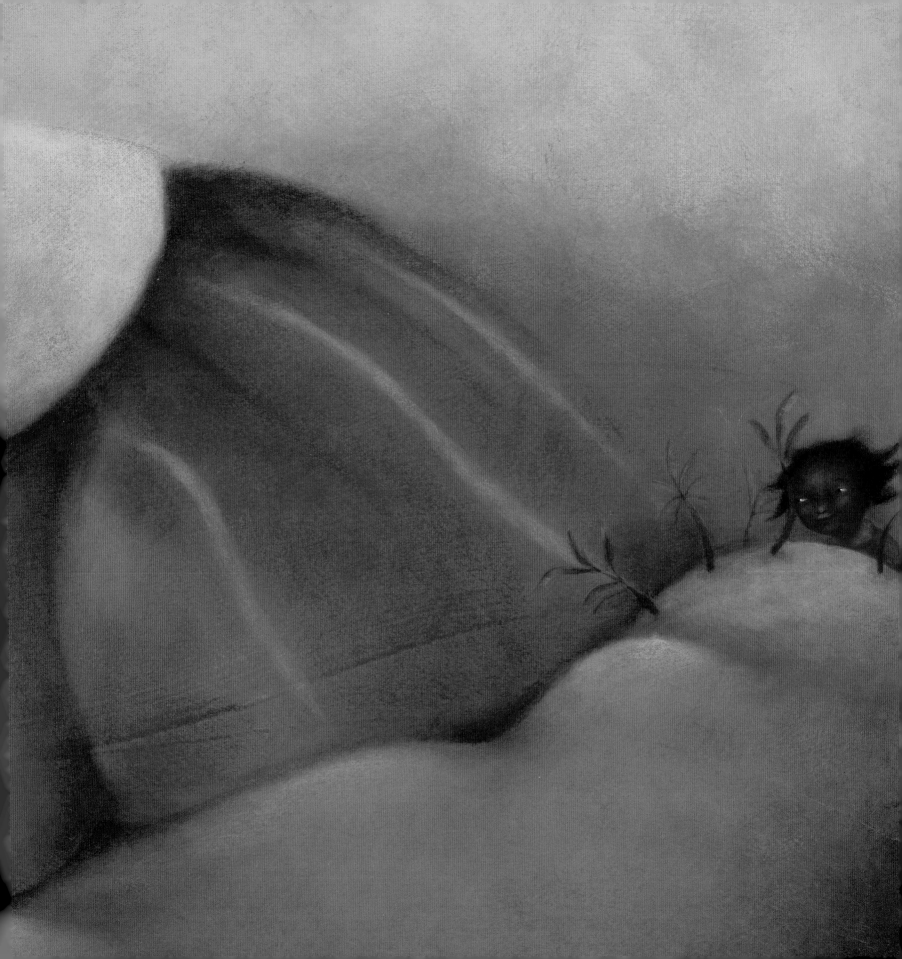

"Hmmm,"
Mother Sky looks down
a rabbit hole. She puts her cheek on
the darkest sand. When she peeks behind
the hills, whom does she see?

⁓

—Mmm . . . —Madre Cielo mira dentro de la
madriguera del conejo. Acerca la mejilla a la oscura arena.
Cuando mira más allá de las colinas, ¿a quién ve?

"I found you, I found my
Little Night."
     Face scrub, lather up, towel
spread, and catch Little Night
in the air.

❧

—Te encontré, encontré a mi
Nochecita.
     Cara limpia, pompas de jabón,
y con la toalla extendida arropa
a Nochecita en el aire.

As the sun sets, so red, Mother Sky unfolds a dress crocheted from
clouds and calls, "Dressing time for Little Night!"
Little Night hops out of her chair, "Not now, not yet, not until you
find me, Mama. Don't forget to close your eyes!"

Cae el sol, y el cielo se tiñe de rojo.
Madre Cielo elige un vestido tejido de nubes
de algodón y anuncia:
—¡Es hora de vestir a Nochecita!
Nochecita salta de la silla.
—Todavía no. Primero tienes
que encontrarme, Mami.
¡No olvides taparte los ojos!

"Where could you be?"
Mother Sky hovers by the shade of trees. She searches in the stripes of bees. When she peeks inside the bats' cave, whom does she see?

—¿Dónde estarás?
Madre Cielo sobrevuela la sombra de los árboles. Busca entre las rayas de las abejas. Cuando se asoma a la cueva de los murciélagos, ¿a quién ve?

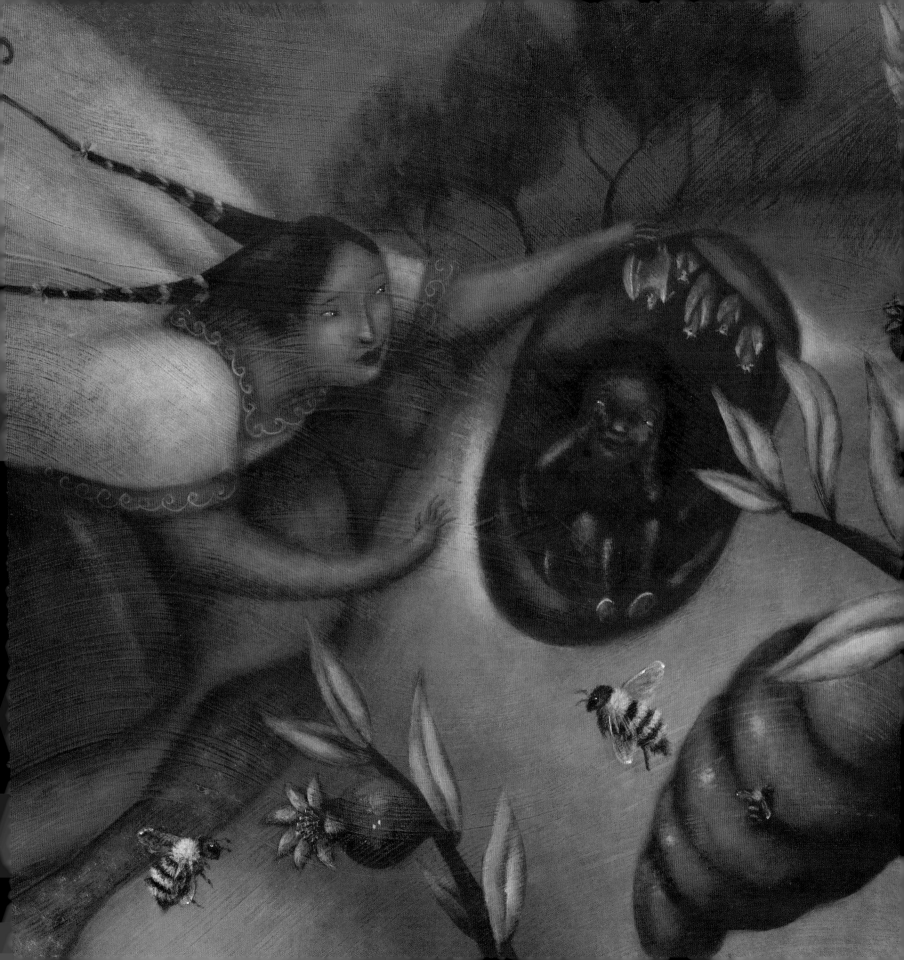

"I found you, I found my Little Night."
Two arms in, one head out, button the
dress crocheted from clouds.

～

—Te encontré, encontré a mi Nochecita.
Dentro los dos brazos, fuera la cabeza,
ciñe el vestido tejido de nubes de algodón.

As the warm of the day fades, Mother Sky fills up a glass of milk and serves pancakes on a plate. She calls, "Time to eat, Little Night!"

Little Night dashes past the table. "Count first, Mama, from one to ten. It is going to be hard to find me this time!"

Cuando el calor del día se desvanece, Madre Cielo llena un vaso de leche y prepara un plato con tortitas.

—¡Es hora de comer, Nochecita! —llama. Nochecita sale corriendo.

—Cuenta primero, Mami, del uno al diez. ¡Esta vez será difícil que me encuentres!

Mother Sky counts, "One, two, three . . .

"Let's see," Mother Sky looks inside the old barn. She pats the raven chicks. When she brushes her hand over the blueberry field, whom does she see?

Madre Cielo cuenta: «Uno, dos, tres . . . ».

—¡Voy! —Madre Cielo busca dentro del viejo granero. Acaricia los polluelos del cuervo. Cuando pasa la mano sobre el campo de arándanos, ¿a quién ve?

"I found you, I found my
Little Night."
Creamy mustache, lips lick, stars
dripping from the Milky Way to drink.

~

—Te encontré, encontré a mi Nochecita.
Bigotes cremosos, labios relamidos,
la Vía Láctea gotea sabrosas estrellas
de leche para beber.

As fireflies and moths come out, Mother Sky sits
on her rocking chair, waving her comb. She calls,
"Time to comb your hair, Little Night."
    But what does she hear? Only the hushing of the
balmy wind.

Cuando salen las luciérnagas y las mariposas nocturnas,
Madre Cielo se sienta en su mecedora y agita el peine.
    —¡Es hora de peinarse, Nochecita! —llama.
    ¿Pero qué escucha? Solo el murmullo de la brisa perfumada.

Mother Sky looks around, but Little Night is
not peeking from behind the hills, nor is she
hiding in the cave, nor vanishing into the field.
"Where could my Little Night be?"

❦

Madre Cielo busca aquí y allá, pero no ve a
Nochecita curioseando detrás de las colinas,
ni escondida en la cueva, ni oculta en el campo.
—¿Dónde está mi Nochecita?

"Peekaboo, Mama.
I am right here!"

—¡Buu, Mami!
¡Estoy aquí!

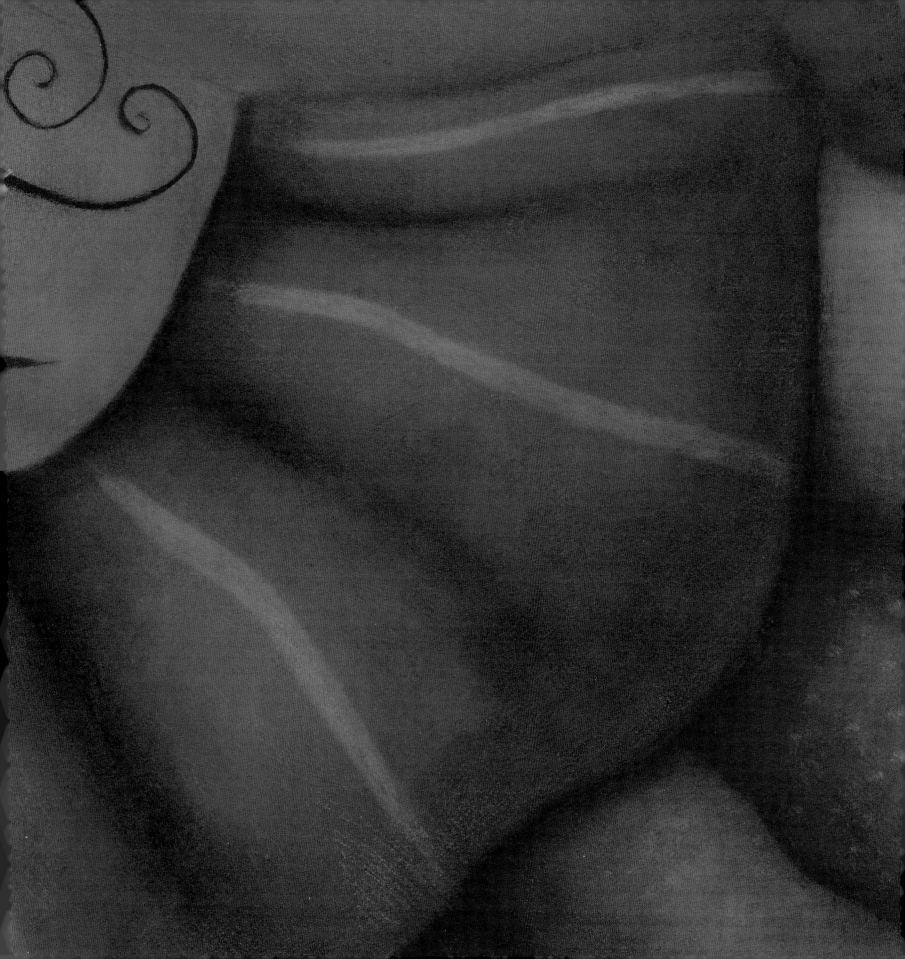

Mother Sky sits Little Night on
her lap and with her shiny comb she
untangles the knots, twists the hair
between her fingers, and makes little swirls,
one on the left side, one on the right side.

Madre Cielo sienta a Nochecita en su regazo
y con su reluciente peine le desenreda las marañas,
y le ensortija el pelo con los dedos, modelando ricitos,
uno en el lado izquierdo y otro en el lado derecho.

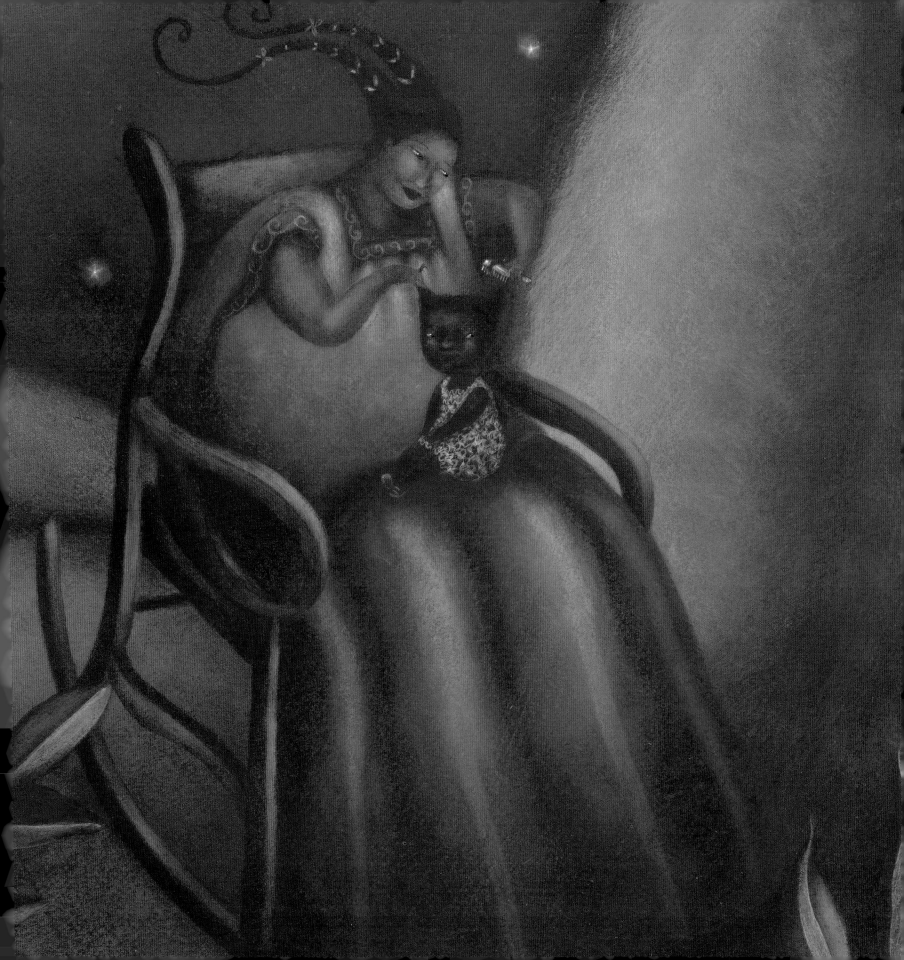

To keep them in place
she takes three hairpins
from her pocket.
"Venus is on the east, Mercury
on the west, and Jupiter above."

Para sujetarlos saca tres
pasadores de su bolsillo.
—Venus está al Este, Mercurio,
al Oeste, y Júpiter, arriba.

"Now, my Little Night, take your
moon ball and play."
"I can catch it, Mama. See me
bounce it high into the air!"

⌇

—Ahora, mi querida Nochecita,
toma tu pelota de luna y ve a jugar.
—Yo puedo atraparla, Mami.
¡Mira cómo rebota en el aire!

In the flowered city there is an endless mother,
giving and magnificent like the sky.
She is my mother, Eloina. This book is for her.

Note: While making this book, I met two brave mothers,
who, like many Mexican women, are fighting cancer and poverty
to keep alive. They have young children to love and raise, and
they work hard every day to stay with them. Señora Badillo
y Asunción, thank you for keeping me inspired.

En la ciudad de flores hay una madre eterna,
generosa y grandiosa como el cielo.
Es Eloina, mi madre. Este libro es para ella.

Nota de la autora: Mientras trabajaba en este libro,
conocí a dos mujeres valientes que, como muchas otras mujeres
mexicanas, luchan contra el cáncer y la pobreza día a día.
Tienen hijos pequeños a quienes brindarles su amor y cuidado
y trabajan con ahínco para seguir a su lado. Gracias, señora
Badillo y Asunción, por inspirarme.

SQUARE
FISH

An Imprint of Macmillan
175 Fifth Avenue
New York, NY 10010
mackids.com

Our books may be purchased in bulk for promotional, educational, or business use. Please contact your local bookseller
or the Macmillan Corporate and Premium Sales Department at (800) 221-7945 ext. 5442 or by e-mail at MacmillanSpecialMarkets@macmillan.com.
Library of Congress Cataloging-in-Publication Data
Morales, Yuyi.
Little Night / written and illustrated by Yuyi Morales.
p. cm.
"A Neal Porter Book."
Summary: At the end of a long day, Mother Sky helps her playful daughter, Little Night, to get ready for bed.
ISBN 978-1-250-07324-2 (paperback)
[1. Bedtime—Fiction. 2. Mothers and daughters—Fiction. 3. Night—Fiction. 4. Sky—Fiction.]
I. Title. II. Title: Nochecita.
PZ73.M7155 2006
[E]—dc22
2006011571

Originally published in the United States by Neal Porter Books/Roaring Brook Press
First Square Fish Edition: 2016
Translation Consultant: Teresa Mlawer
Book designed by Jennifer Browne
Square Fish logo designed by Filomena Tuosto

3 5 7 9 10 8 6 4 2